# Young Cam Jansen
## and the 100th Day of School Mystery

by David A. Adler
illustrated by Susanna Natti

Penguin Young Readers
An Imprint of Penguin Group (USA)

# Chapter 1
## The "Click!" Trick

"Cam! Eric!" Mrs. Wayne called.

"Please, help Maria."

Mrs. Wayne hurried across the hall with Maria.

"These are Cam Jansen and Eric Shelton," she told Maria.

"You're in their class."

"Hello," Cam and Eric said.

"This is Maria's first day," Mrs. Wayne said.

"I have no time to take her to class.

I must get back to the office."

Cam said, "We'll take her to

Ms. Dee's class."

Mrs. Wayne thanked Cam and Eric.

Then she hurried to the office.

"Mrs. Wayne is the principal's

secretary," Eric said.

"She's always busy."

"This may be your first day," Cam told

Maria, "but it's the 100th day for us.

We're having a party."

Cam and Eric took Maria to class.

"Look at all the balloons," Eric said.

"They are all purple or pink because we're having a Letter P party.

Everything for the party will start with the letter P.

I think we'll be eating pretzels, popcorn, and maybe pizza."

Cam said, "Kindergarten is having a Letter A party.

They're having animal crackers
and apple juice."
Maria asked, "Why is every class
having a letter party?"
"That was Dr. Prell's idea," Cam said.
"She's the principal,
and she loves to read.
Dr. Prell says letters make words.
Words make sentences and stories."
"And we read stories," Eric said.
Ms. Dee gave Maria
a desk near Cam, Eric, and Danny.
Danny asked, "Did Cam show you
her 'Click!' trick?"
Cam looked at Danny.
She said, "Click!" and closed her eyes.

A P
N
K
L
D
Y I R
E
S

"Am I wearing a belt?" Danny asked.

"Yes," Cam answered.

"It's blue with pictures of sailboats. Each sailboat has two red flags."

"How did she remember all that?" Maria asked.

Cam opened her eyes.

Eric told Maria, "It's like she has a camera in her head.

Cam says, 'Click!' because that's the sound a camera makes."

Cam's real name is Jennifer.

But when people found out about her great memory, they called her "the Camera."

Soon "the Camera" became "Cam."

The bell rang.

"Good morning," Dr. Prell said.

She was in her office.

She spoke into a microphone connected to wires and speakers.

Everyone in the school heard her.

"Now please," Dr. Prell said, "stand for the pledge to our flag."

# Chapter 2
## Now It's Time to Party

The children stood.

They said the pledge.

Dr. Prell made a few more

announcements.

Then she said, "Happy 100th day."

"Wow!" Ms. Dee said.

"Let's see how much 100 is.

Let's sit quietly for 100 seconds."

Ms. Dee looked at her watch.

The class was quiet.

"Are we done yet?" Danny asked.

"No," Ms. Dee said.

"That was just 40 seconds.

We'll start over."

Ms. Dee looked at her watch.

The class was quiet.

Danny looked at Ms. Dee.

He looked at Cam, Eric, and Maria.

He looked at the ceiling.

"That's it," Ms. Dee said at last.

"That's all?" Danny said.

"To me, it seemed like a week!"

Ms. Dee showed the class pictures

from 100 years ago.

"100 years ago," she said,

"there was no television.

There were no computers."

Ms. Dee gave a math lesson

on the number 100.

Then Ms. Dee smiled.

"Now it's time," she said,

"for our 100th day party."

# Chapter 3
## No Pizza!

Ms. Dee opened bags of popcorn
and pretzels.

She asked Cam, Eric, and Maria
to go to the kitchen and get
the other Letter P foods.

"Cam and I know where everything
is," Eric told Maria.

They walked through the cafeteria
to the kitchen.

In the kitchen were two boxes.

"There's pizza," Maria said.

"That must be for us."

She opened one of the boxes.

"Hey," she said. "It's not here!"

Cam, Eric, and Maria opened the other box.

It was also empty.

Eric said, "We'll ask Mrs. Apple. She's the cook.

This is her kitchen."

They found Mrs. Apple in the gym teacher's office.

"We're from Ms. Dee's class," Eric said.

"We can't find the pizza."

"They're having a Letter P party,"

Mrs. Apple told Mr. Day,

the gym teacher.

"They're having pizza

and pineapple juice.

Mr. Baker's class is having

a Letter C party.

They're having carrots, cupcakes,

and cherry soda."

Eric said, "The pizza boxes

are empty."

"Of course the boxes are empty,"

Mrs. Apple said.

"The three pizzas are in the oven."

Cam, Eric, and Maria

followed Mrs. Apple to the kitchen.

Mrs. Apple put on pot-holder gloves.

She opened the oven.

The oven was empty.

# Chapter 4
## Who Doesn't Like Noodles and Corn?

Mrs. Apple shook her head.

"I know the pizza was in the oven,"

she said.

"I put it there."

Mrs. Apple thought for a moment.

"Oh," she said.

"Then I took it out

and put it on these racks."

The racks were on the counter.

There was no pizza on the racks.

"Could you have put it somewhere

else?" Maria asked.

Mrs. Apple thought for a moment.

"Maybe," she said.

"Lots of times I put things

in the refrigerator or freezer.

Maybe I put the pizza there.

Maybe I put it in the pantry."

Cam opened the refrigerator.

She found pineapple juice, apple
juice, and milk.

Mrs. Apple said, "The apple juice
is for the kindergarten."

Eric opened the freezer.

He found two large containers
of maple walnut ice cream.

Mrs. Apple said, "The maple walnut
ice cream is for Mr. Tate's class.

They're having a Letter M party."

Maria opened the pantry.

She found boxes of noodles

and cans of tomato sauce and corn.

"That's for lunch," Mrs. Apple said.

Maria laughed.

"Now I know who took the pizza,"

she said.

"It was someone who doesn't like

today's lunch.

It was someone who doesn't like

noodles and corn."

# Chapter 5
## That's It!

"Everyone likes my lunches,"

Mrs. Apple said.

Maria said, "Then maybe the gym

teacher ate the pizza. Gym teachers

jump a lot.

Jumping would make him hungry."

"No," Mrs. Apple said.

"Mr. Day wouldn't take anything

that wasn't his."

Mrs. Apple opened the refrigerator.

"Take the pineapple juice to your class," she said.

"Please, tell Ms. Dee I'm sorry. I shouldn't have left the kitchen. Tell her I'll order more pizza."

Cam, Eric, and Maria each took a can of pineapple juice.

"Cam solves mysteries," Eric told Maria as they walked to class.

"I bet she'll solve this one and find the missing pizza."

Cam, Eric, and Maria gave Ms. Dee
the pineapple juice.

Eric told her about the pizza.

Danny gave everyone a paper plate
and cup.

Ms. Dee gave them popcorn,
pretzels, and pineapple juice.

Cam nibbled popcorn and
looked at Ms. Dee.

She looked at all the letters
of the alphabet on the wall
behind Ms. Dee.

"That's it!" Cam said.

She closed her eyes and said,
"Click!"

Cam looked at a picture
she had in her head.

Then Cam opened her eyes
and said, "I know where to find
the missing pizza."

# Chapter 6
## Messy Pizza

"Where?" Eric asked.

Cam hurried to the front of the room.

She told Ms. Dee,

"I have to go to Mr. Baker's class.

I think they have our pizza."

Eric and Maria said,

"We want to go, too."

Eric and Maria followed Cam

out of the room.

Eric asked, "How do you know the

pizza is in Mr. Baker's class?"

Cam stopped.

"What was in the refrigerator?"

she asked.

"Cold things," Maria answered.

"Yes," Cam said.

"There was apple juice for the

Letter A party.

There was pineapple juice for the

Letter P party.

There was milk for the Letter M party.

Mr. Baker's class is having

a Letter C party.

Where was their cherry soda?"

Eric and Maria didn't know.

"The children from Mr. Baker's class took the cherry soda.

I think they also took the pizza."

Cam said, "Mrs. Apple told us there were three pizzas.

But there were only two pizza boxes.

They must have put the three pizzas into one of the boxes and taken it."

"But pizza is a Letter P food," Eric said.

On Mr. Baker's desk was a pizza box.

"Are you in Ms. Dee's class?"

Mr. Baker asked.

"Yes," Eric told him.

"This pizza is yours," Mr. Baker said.

"I was just about to have someone

take it to your room."

More than 20 pizza slices

were jammed in the one pizza box.

"I'm sorry," Mr. Baker said.

"I sent three students to the kitchen.

I said, 'Bring back the Letter C
drinks and foods.'
They brought back cupcakes,
cherry soda, and pizza."
Maria said, "But pizza starts with P."
"Yes," Cam said.
"But cheese begins with C,
and pizza has lots of cheese."
Eric went to the kitchen.
He told Mrs. Apple they had found
the pizza.

Eric met Cam and Maria in the hall.

He helped them carry the messy box

to Ms. Dee's room.

"Oh my," Ms. Dee said when she

opened it.

"This is a mess!"

She put pizza on a plate.

Danny said, "I'll take that.

I like messy food."

Soon everyone in Ms. Dee's class

was eating messy pizza.

Ms. Dee's class had a happy,

messy 100th day party.

# A Cam Jansen Memory Game

Take another look at the picture on page 30.
Study it.
Blink your eyes and say, "Click!"
Then turn back to this page
and answer these questions:

1. Is Cam holding a plate of pizza?

2. How many pizza boxes are on Ms. Dee's desk?

3. In the picture, are there more pink balloons or more purple balloons?

4. Is anyone in the picture wearing eyeglasses?

5. What color is Cam's shirt?

Dear Parents and Educators,

Welcome to Penguin Young Readers! As parents and educators, you
know that each child develops at his or her own pace—in terms of
speech, critical thinking, and, of course, reading. Penguin Young
Readers recognizes this fact. As a result, each Penguin Young Readers
book is assigned a traditional easy-to-read level (1–4) as well as a
Guided Reading Level (A–P). Both of these systems will help you choose
the right book for your child. Please refer to the back of each book
for specific leveling information. Penguin Young Readers features
esteemed authors and illustrators, stories about favorite characters,
fascinating nonfiction, and more!

## Young Cam Jansen and the 100th Day of School Mystery

LEVEL **3**

GUIDED
READING
LEVEL **J**

This book is perfect for a **Transitional Reader** who:
- can read multisyllable and compound words;
- can read words with prefixes and suffixes;
- is able to identify story elements (beginning, middle, end, plot, setting, characters, problem, solution); and
- can understand different points of view.

Here are some **activities** you can do during and after reading this book:
- Problem/Solution: The problem in this story is that the pizza for Cam's class party is missing! How does Cam solve the mystery? What happened to the pizza?
- Make Connections: The 100th day of school is celebrated in many classrooms. Discuss the ways the child has celebrated this day. Also, if the child were to throw a party for the 100th day of school, what would he or she do?

Remember, sharing the love of reading with a child is the best gift
you can give!

—Bonnie Bader, EdM
   Penguin Young Readers program

*Penguin Young Readers are leveled by independent reviewers applying the standards developed by Irene Fountas and Gay Su Pinnell in *Matching Books to Readers: Using Leveled Books in Guided Reading*, Heinemann, 1999.